Contents

The Spy in the Attic

by Ursel Scheffler
illustrated by Christa Unzner

translated by Marianne Martens

North-South Books
New York / London

GALWAY COUNTY LIBRARIES

Copyright © 1997 by Nord-Süd Verlag AG, Gossau Zürich, Switzerland.
First published in Switzerland under the title *Der Spion unterm Dach*.
English translation copyright © 1997 by North-South Books Inc.

All rights reserved.
No part of this book may be reproduced or utilized in any form
or by any means, electronic or mechanical, including photocopying,
recording, or any information storage and retrieval system,
without permission in writing from the publisher.

First published in the United States, Great Britain, Canada,
Australia, and New Zealand in 1997 by North-South Books,
an imprint of Nord-Süd Verlag AG, Gossau Zürich, Switzerland.

Distributed in the United States by North-South Books Inc., New York.

Library of Congress Cataloging-in-Publication Data is available.
A CIP catalogue record for this book is available from The British Library.
ISBN 1-55858-727-6 (trade binding) 10 9 8 7 6 5 4 3 2 1
ISBN 1-55858-728-4 (library binding) 10 9 8 7 6 5 4 3 2 1
Printed in Belgium

For more information about our books, and the authors and artists
who create them, visit our web site: http://www.northsouth.com

1. A Mysterious Delivery

It was late at night, and most of the people at number 7 Maple Street were already sound asleep. But Martin Pitman couldn't sleep. He had eaten too many salty peanuts that evening and now he was dying of thirst. On his way to the kitchen to get a drink of water, he heard a noise out in the street.

He ran to the window.

A truck was parked in front of the house. Two men in overalls got out. They opened the back of the truck and unloaded some odd-looking things. Then they dragged them to the front of the building. Who would be getting a delivery in the middle of the night? Martin heard the men's work boots clomping up the stairs.

Martin ran to the front door. He was just big enough to look through the peephole in the door. He could look through it without being seen from the outside. The men walked by the door. They both had dark hair, and one had a beard. Martin pressed his nose against the door to see as much as he could. The steps grew distant.

Martin crept into the stairwell. He could hear the deliverymen talking. They were speaking a language that he couldn't understand.

They stopped at the attic apartment of the strange man who had moved in a few days ago. Martin had seen him around. He always wore gloves and sunglasses.

Pretty suspicious, thought Martin. Martin was crazy about mysteries and spy stories.

Who knew what was going on up in the attic?

After a while, Martin heard the stairs creaking. All three men were on their way back down! Quick! Get back inside! Martin watched them through the peephole as they went by. Wow, this was exciting!

Martin ran back to the window. The men were unloading a black box that looked like a coffin. They brought it into the house. Martin ran back into the stairwell. The men huffed and puffed, carrying the coffin past Martin's door. Martin could see only the tops of their heads. He couldn't see the coffin. What would the man in the attic need a coffin for? And why would he have it delivered in the middle of the night? This was getting more and more suspicious!

Unfortunately, Martin couldn't see all the things being unloaded. But he did see a long shiny tube that looked like a cannon.

Perhaps the man in the attic was a gun runner!

Finally the noises on the stairs stopped. The truck was empty. The men stood for a while in front of the house talking. Once in a while the glow from the end of a cigarette lit up.

One of the men stood with his hands
in his pockets, looking up at the
windows of the house. Martin ducked,
as quick as lightning. I hope they didn't
see me, he thought.

Maybe the man in the attic was a secret agent or a spy! Spies were dangerous. They took photos with cameras hidden in their coats! They hid secret messages in their shoes. Martin knew all about this from detective stories. He shivered.

He jumped into his bed. His feet were ice cold. He had completely forgotten about the drink of water.

2. The Detectives Gather

Just one floor below Martin Pitman, his friend Pauline Conner had slept through all the action of the night before.

Martin went to the Conners' place every morning to pick up Pauline for school. Today he couldn't wait to tell her the news, and got there ten minutes earlier than usual.

The Conners were still eating breakfast. "Guess what," he said. "Last night the man living in the attic apartment had some weird stuff delivered!"

"The man is called Mr. Leon," said Mrs. Conner. "He put his name on the buzzer downstairs yesterday."

"That's because he was expecting someone!" said Martin.

"And how do you know about the delivery?" asked Pauline's father.

"I couldn't sleep last night," said Martin. "So I saw everything. And it was very suspicious, if you ask me!"

"Sounds to me like you've been reading too many detective novels," said Mr. Conner, biting into his toast.

"Leon is a funny name," said Pauline.

"It's a Spanish name. It means lion," said Pauline's father.

"So what if he's Spanish?" said Martin. "That still doesn't explain why he would get deliveries in the middle of the night, does it?"

"Why not? If his furniture was shipped from Spain, perhaps the movers couldn't get here any sooner," said Pauline's mother thoughtfully. "Who knows? Maybe they hit heavy traffic or perhaps there was an accident. Anything could have happened."

"But those weren't just ordinary movers," Martin mumbled. "And they weren't delivering ordinary furniture, either!"

"Come on, kids, time for school!" Mr. Conner said. "It's already ten minutes to eight!"

Martin and Pauline sprinted down the stairs. When they got to the bottom, it was seven minutes to eight.

"I'll bet you the man's a spy," said Martin as they turned the corner by their school. "Why else would he have a cannon?"

"A cannon? Maybe he hunts sparrows!" Pauline giggled.

"Very funny," said Martin. "We'd better keep an eye on him. Something is up with that man. He's got to be a spy."

"I don't know," said Pauline. "I saw him only once, in the supermarket. He was wearing sunglasses and gloves. And carrying a cane."

"Disguises, disguises, disguises," said Martin knowingly. "I once saw a film where the spy hid a weapon in his cane."

"Spies know all the tricks," said Pauline. "Uh-oh, there's the bell. We'd better run for it!"

That afternoon, Martin and Pauline told their friends Philip and Julia all about their exciting observations.

"Eight eyes can see more than four eyes," said Martin. "You can help. Do you want to be our assistant detectives?"

"Of course," said Julia. "I even have binoculars from my grandfather."

"And I have a magnifying glass, from my stamp collection," said Philip.

"Great!" said Martin. "Keep your eyes and ears open. And be careful he doesn't spot you shadowing him."

3. Spying on the Spy

Later that day, Julia was the first one to spot the spy. "Look! There he is, buying a paper!" she whispered, grabbing Martin's sleeve. "Use the binoculars!"

"Aha! Our secret agent got himself a dog," said Martin, whistling through his teeth.

"Perhaps it's a bomb-sniffing dog," said Philip.

"He's not very big, and he looks like a mongrel. But he does seem intelligent," Martin reported, pressing the binoculars to his eyes. "He just peed on the drainpipe by the flower shop."

"What's so intelligent about that?" asked Pauline.

Martin ignored her. "Leon just bought a newspaper," he reported. "And now the dog is carrying the paper for him. A stupid dog wouldn't be able to do that."

"Watch out! They're coming!" warned Julia.

They ducked into an alley and watched as Mr. Leon and his dog went by.

The dog was carrying a Spanish newspaper. Mr. Leon was wearing his hat, his sunglasses, and his gloves.

"How can he wear gloves in this heat?" Julia said. "He's nuts!"

"Because of fingerprints, of course," Pauline whispered.

"Did you hear that? Mr. Leon just said, 'Sit, Watson!' to his dog," said Philip excitedly. "I heard him loud and clear."

The dog sat nicely at the corner and waited until the cars had passed. Then he crossed the street with Mr. Leon.

"Do you think the dog is named after Dr. Watson in Sherlock Holmes?" asked Martin.

Philip nodded.

"A Spanish secret agent who has a dog named after an English detective's friend. That is odd," said Martin. "This case gets more and more interesting."

4. A Scary Package

They didn't see Mr. Leon the next day, not on the way to school, and not on the way home.

"It's like the earth swallowed him up or something!" said Julia.

"Do you think he's moved away?" said Philip.

"My mother said that he took his dog out yesterday evening," said Pauline. "And he greeted her very politely."

"That's all just part of his cover," said Martin.

When Martin got home, there was a large package sitting in the Pitmans' front hall.

"This—this is addressed to the man upstairs!" Martin spluttered.

"Why, yes," said his mother. "What's wrong with that? Mr. Leon wasn't home, so the postman left it here."

Mother is clueless, Martin thought. "What if there's a bomb in there?" he said.

"Martin, you really have an overactive imagination," said his mother.

"But listen—I hear something ticking!" said Martin.

His mother pressed her ear against the package.

And then she turned pale.

Something really *was* ticking in the package.

"Should I call the police, or the firemen?" asked Martin.

GALWAY COUNTY LIBRARIES

Just then the doorbell rang. Martin and his mother stared at the door. Mother opened it slowly.

There stood Mr. Leon, the spy!

"The postman left a note in my mailbox," said Mr. Leon. "Thanks for taking my package for me."

"Watch out! There's a bomb in there," Martin wanted to say, but the words stuck in his throat.

And then, when Mr. Leon bent down to pick up the package, his hair slid to one side!

Gosh—a wig! thought Martin. Now that's what I call a disguise! I can't wait to tell the others. And he raced downstairs to see Pauline.

Pauline was very impressed when Martin told her about the wig and the package with the bomb. But then nothing else happened. For three days no one saw Mr. Leon.

"Maybe the package blew up in his face," said Martin.

"If a bomb had exploded, we all would have heard it," said Julia.

"Maybe there were poisoned chocolates inside," suggested Philip.

"Or poisoned gas," said Pauline.

5. A Dangerous Mission

The next day, when Martin came home from school, he found his mother talking to Dr. Jones.

"We'll take care of him," Mrs. Pitman was saying.

Dr. Jones turned to Martin. "Martin," he said, "I'm glad I ran into you. Perhaps you could take Mr. Leon's dog for a walk? He is sick."

"Poor dog!" said Martin.

"No, Mr. Leon is sick. That's why he can't take his dog out."

"Of course. Martin will be happy to do that," said Mrs. Pitman.

Martin protested, but his mother insisted that they go straight up to Mr. Leon.

Mr. Leon was lying in bed. And his wig had slid off to the side again.

"I had a terrible car accident not so long ago," he explained. "And then the move . . . I think it's all been a bit too much for me. So now I'm stuck in bed."

"I'll bring you something to eat so you can get your strength back," said Mrs. Pitman. "And Martin will take your dog out."

"You are all very kind," said Mr. Leon.

Martin took Watson the dog and ran downstairs. He rang Pauline's doorbell and told her the latest news.

"I'm not taking some secret agent's dog out for a walk," said Pauline.

"Why not?" said Martin. "When we bring the dog back to him, we'll have the perfect opportunity to case his place."

Watson had a great time with the children.

"Not a bad dog, really," said Martin.

"I guess it's not his fault that his owner is a spy," Pauline mumbled, scratching Watson behind his ears.

"Let's take him out again tomorrow," Pauline suggested. "Will you pick me up?"

"Of course," said Martin. "But now comes the dangerous part. We have to take Watson back home."

"Are you coming up with me?" asked Martin as they arrived at the first floor.

Pauline nodded.

Mrs. Pitman was waiting for them on the second floor.

"What took you so long?" she shouted at them. "Mr. Leon was getting worried! I was just upstairs. Here is his key. That way he won't have to get out of bed to let you in."

Watson sprinted happily upstairs.

Martin and Pauline walked a lot slower.

"Here we go, into the lion's den," Pauline whispered.

"I'm a little scared," said Martin. He opened the door.

6. Into the Lion's Den

Mr. Leon thanked Martin and Pauline for taking Watson out. He told them that he had injured his head when he had the car accident. "I'm wearing this wig just until my hair grows back," he said.

"Do you travel a lot by car?" asked Martin.

"Well, yes, my job requires it," said Mr. Leon.

"Are you a racing car driver?" asked Pauline.

"Oh, no!" said Mr. Leon, laughing. "I'm a musician, and I travel a lot. I hope to be able to play again soon."

He pointed to his piano.

Martin recognized the black box that he had thought was a coffin, and turned bright red.

"You have to wear gloves because . . ." Pauline began.

"I also injured my hands in the crash." At that moment the alarm clock on the bedside table rang.

Mr. Leon grabbed it and said: "It's really old-fashioned, isn't it? I ordered it because it's hard for me to set my radio alarm with my injured hands."

"So that was what was in that package!" Martin said, embarrassed.

"That's right," said Mr. Leon. "I have to set it several times a day so that I don't forget to take my medicine."

Watson came running. He wagged his tail and jumped up on the bed.

"You're the greatest," said Mr. Leon, scratching his head. "He's a very loyal friend. Well, of course I also have millions of faraway friends—the stars!" Mr. Leon smiled.

Carefully he stood up and put on his dressing gown. Then he opened the door to the next room.

"The cannon!" said Martin.

"What did you say?" asked Mr. Leon.

"Oh, er, nothing," said Martin shyly.

"Wow, a real telescope," said Pauline, impressed.

"Can you see the moon with it?" asked Martin.

"The moon, and much more! Come up tonight. If the sky is clear, the moon will seem close enough to touch."

Martin and Pauline were very curious. After dinner, they went up to visit the "spy" upstairs. Mr. Leon told them all about the planets and about stars that were hundreds of light-years away.

He told them the names of the seas on the moon. He showed them the North Star and the Milky Way.

Pauline and Martin looked far out into the universe. But they also took a fresh look at what was right next to them—their new friend, Mr. Leon.

ABOUT THE AUTHOR

Ursel Scheffler was born in Nuremberg, a German city where many toys are made. She has written over one hundred children's books, which have been published in fifteen different languages. Her other easy-to-read books for North-South are a trio of adventures featuring a sly fox and a duck detective: *Rinaldo, the Sly Fox*; *The Return of Rinaldo, the Sly Fox*; and *Rinaldo on the Run*.

ABOUT THE ILLUSTRATOR

Christa Unzner was born in a town near Berlin, Germany. She had always wanted to be a ballet dancer, but she ended up studying commercial art and working in an advertising agency.

Winning third prize in a book illustration contest led her to a career as a free-lance illustrator, primarily of children's books. Her previous easy-to-read books for North South are *Loretta and the Little Fairy* by Gerda Marie Scheidl and *Jasmine and Rex* by Wolfram Hänel.